W9-BRK-777

MEET CHADWICK
AND HIS
CHESAPEAKE BAY FRIENDS

Frederick County Public Libraries

PURCHASED WITH A
GRANT AWARDED BY

G. Frank Thomas Fund

By Priscilla Cummings

Illustrated by A.R.Cohen

TIDEWATER PUBLISHERS
Centreville, Maryland

Text copyright © 1999 by Priscilla Cummings
Illustrations copyright © 1999 by A.R.Cohen
Printed in China

FREDERICK COUNTY PUBLIC LIBRARIES

If you would like to meet a crab,
A crab with googlie eyes,
Then come along and take a look.
You're in for a surprise!

Meet Chadwick, the Chesapeake Crab,
As happy as can be.
He lives beneath blue waters
In a bay, beside the sea.

He has eight legs to help him swim,
And two big pincers, too.
He swims and pinches all day long.
It's what crabs like to do!

Young Chadwick has a lot of friends
In the bay and on the beach.
Some like the water, some like land,
And some like some of each.

Some friends have noses, some have beaks,
And some of them have bills.
Some friends have feathers, some have fur,
And some of them have gills.

FRIENDS

Meet Bernie, who's a sea gull,
Always looking for some lunch.
He loves a fish at dinnertime
And cookies by the bunch.

Friend Bernie is a fat old bird,
As happy as can be.
He eats his fish and flies above
The bay, beside the sea.

Meet Miss Matilda, white egret—
A proper one at that!
She always looks her very best
With flowers in her hat.

Matilda is a lady bird,
As fussy as can be.
She loves her mucky, muddy marsh
Near the bay, beside the sea.

Now meet Toulouse, the Canada Goose,
Who visits from the north.
He flies back home in spring and says
He likes the back and forth.

And hear Toulouse, the traveling goose,
Honk honking joyously.
He loves to spend his winters
At the bay, beside the sea.

Meet Hector Spector Jellyfish,
The silliest "fish" you'll find.
He goes this way, then that, because
He can't make up his mind!

Watch Hector Spector Jellyfish,
Wishy-washy as can be.
He doesn't know which way to go
In his bay, beside the sea.

Meet Belly Jeans the Flounder,
At the bottom of the bay.
He snuggles underneath the sand
And *there* he wants to stay!

See Belly Jeans the flounder fish,
As splat flat as can be.
He loves life at the bottom
Of the bay, beside the sea.

And now meet Orville Oyster, *shhh!*
It's hard to see his face.
He's very shy and quiet, too,
And stays in just *one* place!

His shell is hard and crusty,
And as solid as can be.
He calls that crusty shell his home
In the bay, beside the sea.

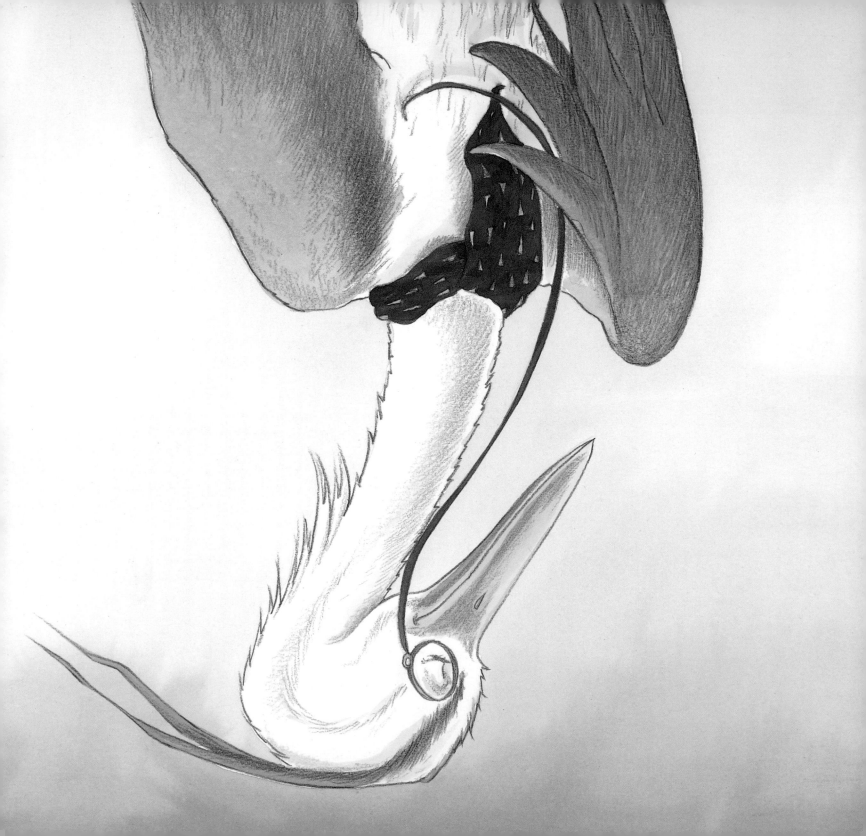

Meet stately Baron von Heron,
So tall and slim and blue.
He can be short when he wants to,
Or tall to see far, too.

The great blue Baron von Heron,
A bird of royalty.
He watches out for all his friends
In the bay, beside the sea.

Meet Sid and Sal, an osprey pair,
Who found a marker best
To build a home and spend their time
In a great big stick-filled nest.

They opened up a diner, too.
Friends eat there frequently.
The food is good at Sid and Sal's,
In the bay, beside the sea.

Meet Esmerelda, lady crab,
With claw tips all in red.
She loves cute Chadwick; he loves her.
That's all that need be said.

So pretty, Esmerelda is—
So happy and so free!
All day she plays with Chadwick
In the bay, beside the sea.

Though Chadwick and his many friends
Are different as can be,
They live together happily
In a bay, beside the sea.

SEP 3 0 2005

S 1982 02037 1989